The NeveR

in a blink

Written by
Kiki Thorpe

Illustrated by
Jana Christy

A STEPPING STONE BOOK™

RANDOM HOUSE 🏠 NEW YORK

For Roxie and Freddie —K.T.
To Sophia Elizabeth from Flanty —J.C.

The publisher would like to thank Caroline Egan for her artistic vision.

Copyright © 2013 Disney Enterprises, Inc. All rights reserved. Published in the United States by Random House Children's Books, a division of Random House, Inc., 1745 Broadway, New York, NY 10019, and in Canada by Random House of Canada Limited, Toronto, in conjunction with Disney Enterprises, Inc. Random House and the colophon are registered trademarks, and A STEPPING STONE BOOK and the colophon are trademarks of Random House, Inc.

Library of Congress Cataloging-in-Publication Data
Thorpe, Kiki.
In a blink/by Kiki Thorpe; illustrated by Jana Christy.
p. cm.—(Disney fairies) (Never girls; 1)
"A Stepping Stone book."
Summary: When four friends are whisked out of their ordinary
lives to Never Land, home to fairies and mermaids, Queen Clarion
and Tinker Bell have to figure out a way for them to get home.
ISBN 978-0-7364-2794-4 (trade) — ISBN 978-0-7364-8137-3 (lib. bdg.)
[1. Fairies—Fiction. 2. Magic—Fiction. 3. Characters in literature—Fiction.]
I. Christy, Jana, ill. II. Title.
PZ7.T3974In 2013
[Fic]—dc23 2012014199
Box ISBN 978-0-593-38118-2 (proprietary edition)
rhcbooks.com
MANUFACTURED IN CHINA
10 9 8 7 6 5 4 3 2 1

Never Land

Far away from the world we know, on the distant seas of dreams, lies an island called Never Land. It is a place full of magic, where mermaids sing, fairies play, and children never grow up. Adventures happen every day, and anything is possible.

There are two ways to reach Never Land. One is to find the island yourself. The other is for it to find you. Finding Never Land on your own takes a lot of luck and a pinch of fairy dust. Even then, you will only find the island if it wants to be found.

Every once in a while, Never Land drifts close to our world . . . so close a fairy's laugh slips through. And every once in an even longer while, Never Land opens its doors to a special few. Believing in magic and fairies from the bottom of your heart can make the extraordinary happen. If you suddenly hear tiny bells or feel a sea breeze where there is no sea, pay careful attention. Never Land may be close by. You could find yourself there in the blink of an eye.

One day, four special girls came to Never Land in just this way. This is their story.

Never Land

Pirate Cove

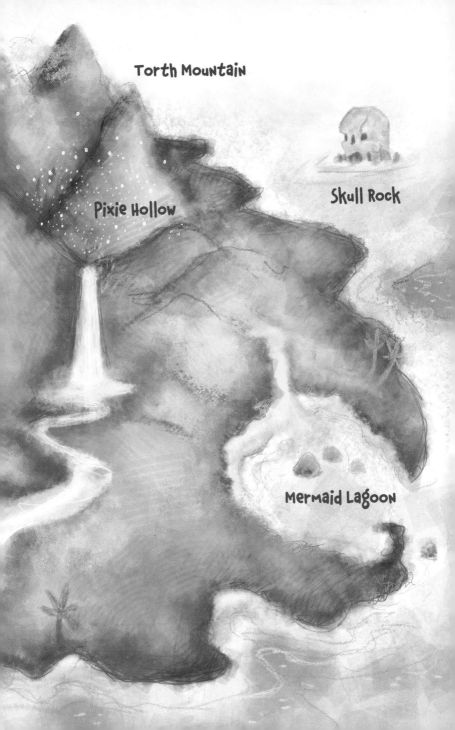

Torth Mountain

Skull Rock

Pixie Hollow

Mermaid Lagoon

Chapter 1

There it was. That sound again.

Kate McCrady froze. The soccer ball rolled past her, but she didn't even notice. She cocked her head to one side, listening.

Yes, it was the same sound she'd been hearing all afternoon. High and silvery, like little bells ringing. Kate looked around the backyard. What could it be?

"I got it!" yelled Lainey Winters. She chased the ball into the corner of the yard. Lainey's big glasses slid down her nose as she scooped up the ball. "I got it!" she cried again. "Kate's the monkey in the middle now!"

Across the lawn, Kate's best friend, Mia Vasquez, put her hands on her hips. "What's the matter, Kate?" she asked. It wasn't like Kate to miss such an easy pass.

"Do you hear that sound?" Kate asked her.

"What sound?" Mia replied.

"What's going on?" called Lainey, feeling left out. "Aren't we playing?"

Kate listened again. She couldn't hear the bells anymore. She felt excited, although she didn't know why. "It was nothing, I guess," she said, turning back to the game.

"You're in the middle now," Mia reminded her.

Kate shrugged. She was good at soccer. She was good at most things that involved running, jumping, kicking, or catching. She was never in the middle for very long.

"Okay, Lainey. You come take my spot," she called. "Lainey! Lainey?"

*

Lainey didn't hear her. She was staring up at the sky. A flock of flamingos was passing overhead.

Flamingos? thought Lainey. *That can't be right.* Lainey's third-grade science book had a picture of a flamingo in it. Flamingos lived in warm, sunny places. They lived near oceans and lakes. They didn't live in cities like Lainey's.

Maybe her glasses were playing tricks on her. Lainey took them off and rubbed

them on her shirt. When she put them back on, the flamingos were gone. Where they'd been, Lainey saw only feathery clouds.

"Lainey!" Mia yelled.

Lainey looked over, startled. "Did you see the flamingos?" she asked.

From the way Kate and Mia stared at her, Lainey could tell she'd said something wrong. She felt her face turn red.

"We're ready to play," said Kate. "But you have the ball."

Lainey looked down at the ball in her arms. "Oh, right." Lainey set the ball down on the grass. She glanced up at the sky one last time. Not a flamingo in sight.

But as the clouds drifted toward the horizon, Lainey could have sworn she heard the sound of flapping wings.

✳

Across the lawn, Mia was growing impatient. Why were her friends acting so funny today? All Mia wanted to do was finish their game!

At last, to Mia's relief, Lainey kicked the ball. *Good*, Mia thought. *No more interruptions.*

But just then the back door of Mia's house slammed open. A small girl in a pink tutu burst outside. She went streaking across the lawn, making a noise like a bumblebee.

"Gabby!" Mia shouted at her little sister. She was headed right for Kate, who was chasing the ball. "Watch out!"

Too late! Gabby slammed into Kate. Both girls tumbled to the ground.

"Gabby!" Mia hollered again, annoyed. "Quit getting in the way."

Gabby sat up. She straightened the costume fairy wings she was wearing. "I wasn't getting in the way," she said. "Kate got in *my* way. I was *flying*."

"You were not flying," Mia said. "You were being a pest."

"It's okay," said Kate, getting up from the grass. "Gabby, do you want to play with us?"

"Yes!" said Gabby at the same moment that Mia said, "No!"

The two sisters glared at each other. "Gabby, you're too little," Mia said in her best big-sister voice. "Go play somewhere else."

Gabby stuck her tongue out at Mia. Then she stomped off toward the flower bed. Gabby liked to play among the flowers, even though she wasn't supposed to.

"Gabby, you leave Mami's flowers alone," Mia said.

Gabby ignored her. She crouched down and examined something in the tulips. "Ooh!" she exclaimed. "A fairy!"

Mia rolled her eyes. Her little sister had a big imagination. But at least she wasn't bugging them anymore. Mia turned back to the game.

At that moment, the wind picked up. Mia caught the smell of seawater. *That's odd*, she thought. She looked around. Something about the way the breeze was blowing made the scrawny trees in her yard sound like rustling palms. Mia had the funny feeling that if she peeked through the fence, she would see the ocean right next door.

Of course, she knew that was crazy.

The ocean was hundreds of miles away.

The wind sent the soccer ball sailing into a corner of the yard. It bent the flowers on their stems and whipped the girls' hair. Above it, Mia could hear a noise like waves crashing on a beach.

The other girls heard it, too. Something strange was happening. They stepped closer together and reached for each other's hands.

"Gabby?" Mia cried, suddenly afraid. "Gabby, come here!"

*

When the fairy appeared in the garden, Gabby was not surprised. She often pretended to talk to fairies. Sometimes she pretended she *was* a fairy. Fairies were so much a part of Gabby's world that it seemed perfectly natural to see one sitting among her mother's tulips.

"Hello, fairy," Gabby said.

"I'm Prilla," said the fairy. "Clap if you believe in fairies!"

No one believed more than Gabby. She clapped her hands hard. Prilla the fairy turned a happy cartwheel in the air.

"I have to go home now," said Prilla.

"Don't go yet!" Gabby cried, just as the wind started to pick up.

The wind was blowing hard. Gabby heard her sister calling, "Gabby? Gabby, come here!"

Because she was afraid Prilla might blow away, Gabby put her hands around her. She held the fairy lightly, cupped in her palms, the way you would hold a butterfly.

And then Mia grabbed her.

The moment Mia touched Gabby, the world blinked. All the girls felt it. It was like the slow click of a camera lens.

The next instant, the backyard was gone.

chapter 2

The girls were standing on an empty beach. Where the fence had been a moment before, waves now curled against a sandy shore. Instead of a house, behind them rose a wall of dense green forest.

A rustling overhead made them look up. A flock of pink flamingos was crossing the sky.

"I *did* see flamingos," Lainey murmured.

"Are we dreaming?" asked Mia.

Kate didn't think it was a dream. She'd

never had a dream so sharp and so clear. But just to be sure, she reached out and pinched Mia.

"Ow!" Mia rubbed her arm. *Kate!*

Kate grinned. "I guess we're not dreaming."

"Mia," Gabby complained, "you're squeezing too hard."

Mia let go of Gabby's arm, which she'd been gripping tightly. Then she noticed Gabby's cupped palms. "What have you got in your hands?" Mia asked.

"A fairy," said Gabby.

"Gabby," said Mia, giving her sister a stern look. "What's the rule about fibbing?"

"But I *do* have a fairy. See?" Gabby opened her hands. A real, live fairy flew out.

The other girls jumped back, startled.

"Oh my gosh!" Mia gasped.

The fairy had curly brown hair and a lemon-yellow glow. She looked as surprised to see the girls as they were to see her. She blinked three times. Then, quick as a wink, she darted away.

"Come back!" Gabby cried.

But the fairy didn't stop. They could see her glow zigzagging between the trees.

Kate turned to her friends. "Well, don't just stand there!" Her heart was pounding with excitement. "Let's follow her!"

*

Prilla raced toward Pixie Hollow, flying as fast as her wings would carry her. Right then she would have given anything to be a fast-flying-talent fairy.

Of course, Prilla thought unhappily, *if I*

were *a fast-flying-talent fairy, I wouldn't be in this mess.*

She rounded a clump of wildflowers and Tinker Bell's workshop came into view. If anyone could help her, it was Tink.

When Prilla burst through the door of the workshop, Tink looked up with a frown. She didn't like to be interrupted while she was working on her pots and pans. But she saw the look on Prilla's face and put down the saucepan she was fixing. "What's wrong?" she asked.

"A problem," Prilla replied. "A big, *big* problem!"

"Well, bring it to me," said Tink. "Whatever it is, I'm sure I can fix it."

"I can't bring it here." Prilla wrung her hands. "Can you come with me?"

"Now?" Tink glanced down at her saucepan. "I was just in the middle of—"

"It's an emergency!" Prilla begged.

Tink sighed. "All right," she said. "What *is* the problem, anyway?"

"I think you need to see this for yourself," said Prilla. Grabbing Tink's hand, she pulled her out the door.

When they reached the beach, Prilla

stopped and hovered in the air. "They were here when I left!" she cried.

"They?" asked Tink.

From far off, the fairies heard a shout. Tink's pointed ears pricked up. "That sounds like Clumsies!"

"That's what I wanted to show you," said Prilla. "Come on."

Prilla and Tink followed the voices into the forest. And then Tink got her first look at Prilla's problem.

Or four problems, to be exact. Four girls were making their way through the trees. The tallest one led the way. She had freckles, a mop of red hair, and a bouncy walk. The girl walking behind her had big glasses that kept sliding down her nose. A girl with long, curly black hair brought up the rear. She held the hand of

a little girl who looked as if she might be her sister. The little girl kept pulling her hand away.

Tink stared. The littlest girl had wings. Tink had never seen a Clumsy with wings before.

"Kate," the girl with glasses said hesitantly, "do you think maybe we're lost?"

The red-haired girl stopped. She put her hands on her hips and looked around. "How can we be lost when we don't even know where we are?" she asked.

"I've never seen these Clumsies before," Tink whispered to Prilla. "Where did they come from?"

"Um . . . ," Prilla said, squirming a little. "Well, you see, I brought them."

"What?" Tink was so shocked her

wings missed a beat. She dropped an inch in the air.

"I didn't mean to," Prilla said quickly. "It was an accident."

Tink pulled on her bangs, as she always did when she was annoyed or confused. Right now, she was both. "Maybe you'd better start from the beginning."

"I was on a blink," Prilla explained. Prilla had an unusual talent, even for a fairy. She could visit children anywhere in the world just by blinking. Prilla's talent was very important. By visiting children, she helped keep their belief in fairies alive. And fairies thrived through children's belief.

Tink nodded. "Go on."

"It was like any other blink, until I

tried to come back," Prilla said. "When I got to Never Land, the girls were here, too! I must have brought them with me!"

"Well, then just blink them back to wherever they came from," said Tink, crossing her arms.

"I tried!" Prilla said. "It didn't work. Oh, Tink, what should I do?"

Tink sighed. This was the trouble with being a fairy who fixed things. Other fairies came to her with all kinds of problems, and not all of them involved pots and pans.

At that moment, the little girl looked up and spotted them. "My fairy's back!" she cried.

"She brought a friend!" the one with glasses said.

The girls scrambled to get a closer look.

"Ooh! See her tiny ponytail?"

"And her little leaf-dress?"

"Look at the pom-poms on her shoes."

"She's sooo cute!"

"I'm not cute!" Tink exclaimed.

Tink had never been very fond of Clumsies (except for Peter Pan, of course), and these girls seemed like a particularly silly bunch. "Prilla, these girls don't belong in Pixie Hollow. Send them home."

"But Tink . . . ," Prilla began.

Just then, they heard the whisper of wings. A third fairy appeared in the glen. It was Spring, a messenger. Prilla and Tink flew over to her.

"Come to the Home Tree at once," Spring told them.

"What is it?" Prilla asked, her heart sinking.

Spring glanced at the four girls. "Bring your Clumsies. The queen wants to have a word with you."

Chapter 3

As the three fairies flew off, Kate scrambled after them. "Quick!" she cried. "Don't let them get away this time!"

The girls chased the fairies through the forest. They ducked under branches. They climbed over fallen logs. They hadn't heard Spring's message and didn't realize that the fairies *wanted* them to follow.

"Where do you think we're going?" Lainey asked, panting a little. The trees were starting to thin out. They could see blue sky up ahead.

"I don't know," Kate said. "But I—"

As Kate stepped into the clearing, her words died on her lips. The other girls came up behind her. They, too, fell silent in wonder.

To understand what the girls felt when they first saw Pixie Hollow, think of your most marvelous dream. Maybe it was filled with soft sunlight or beautiful music or the smell of orange blossoms. Maybe you discovered hidden treasure. Maybe everything felt possible.

For the girls, Pixie Hollow was all those things and more. They were standing at the edge of a meadow thick with wildflowers. And everywhere they looked, they saw fairies.

A fairy rode past on the back of a jackrabbit. Another wove through the air chasing a bright blue butterfly. Fairies darted in and out among the flowers. Their wings sparkled in the sunlight.

Kate started to step forward. Then she drew her foot back with a gasp. A fairy was crossing the ground in front of her. He was riding in a little cart pulled by a mouse. When he saw Kate, he almost fell off his seat in surprise.

The girls made their way slowly through the meadow, being careful where they stepped. Fairies in flower-petal dresses buzzed around them. Soon the girls had drawn a crowd. The fairies kept repeating the same word—"Clumsy."

"Why do they keep saying that?" Mia wondered.

"Maybe they're talking about you," Kate teased.

"I'm not clumsy!" Mia said, offended. She turned to the nearest fairy, saying, "I've had three years of ballet!" The fairy darted away in alarm.

"Oh!" Kate stopped walking so suddenly that the other girls bumped into her. "Look at *that!*"

Ahead stood a maple tree as big as a house. Looking closer, the girls saw that it *was* a house. Tiny doors and windows lined its branches. Several of the windows flew open. Fairies stuck their heads out to stare at the girls.

"Come on! Come on!" The fairies they had been following beckoned to them.

At the base of the great tree was a pebbled courtyard. A fairy stood in the center of it. She wore a long gown made of rose petals. A thin band of gold rested on her head.

"She must be a queen," Mia whispered.

Kate had been leading the way. But now, for the first time, she hesitated. She had never met a queen before. She wasn't sure what to do.

To Kate's astonishment, Gabby stepped in front of her. The little girl held the edges of her tutu and curtsied.

The queen looked pleased. "I am Queen Clarion," she said in a voice that seemed to belong to someone much bigger. "Tell me, why have you come here?"

At last, Kate found her voice. "Your Majesty," she said, stepping forward, "we don't know why we're here. We don't even know *where* we are."

The crowd of fairies tittered. Even the queen seemed surprised. "Why, you're in Pixie Hollow! On the island of Never Land. Are you saying you didn't mean to come?"

"It's my fault." A fairy fluttered forward. It was the one the girls had first seen on the beach.

"Go ahead, Prilla," the queen said.

Prilla explained to the queen what had happened with her blink. "I didn't mean to bring them. I'd fly backward if I could," Prilla added. She was afraid the queen would be angry. No fairy had ever blinked Clumsies to Never Land before.

The queen was quiet for a moment, thinking. "It seems these girls have come here by accident," she said at last. "All the same, we must find a way to get them home. Until then, they will be our guests. Fairies of Pixie Hollow, treat these Clumsies kindly."

"I'm *not* clumsy." Mia spoke up suddenly. "I'm Mia!"

Everyone turned to look at her. Mia blushed, but continued, "That's Kate, and that's Lainey. And this is my little sister, Gabby. We're not clumsy, and I wish you'd stop calling us that . . . er, Your Majesty." She added the last part to be polite.

Silence fell over the courtyard. The queen stared at Mia. Then she laughed. Her laugh was clear and bell-like. As soon as they heard it, the girls relaxed.

"Clumsies are what we call the people of the mainland—*your* world," Queen Clarion explained. "But you're right. While you're our guests, you should be called by your names. Mia, Kate, Lainey, and Gabby, welcome to Pixie Hollow."

The queen clapped her hands. A door in the side of the tree opened and dozens of fairies came out. They were all carrying food—whole strawberries, roasted walnuts, wheels of cheese the size of a penny, loaves of bread no bigger than your thumb . . . and last but not least, four beautiful cakes. It took two fairies each to carry them, although to the girls they were the size of cupcakes.

More fairies unrolled banana leaves to be used as the girls' place mats. Then Kate, Lainey, Mia, and Gabby sat down to their first fairy feast.

Tinker Bell had been watching from the edge of the courtyard. When the girls began to eat, she rose into the air.

Everything was settled. She could get back to her workshop now.

But as she turned to leave, the queen called to her. Tink flew over. "Yes, Queen Clarion?"

"We've never had so many Clumsies in Pixie Hollow," Queen Clarion said.

"No, we haven't," said Tink.

"Taking care of four girls won't be easy, will it?" the queen asked.

"I suppose not," Tink said absently. She was already thinking about her saucepan.

But the queen's next words got her attention. "I want you to help Prilla," the queen told Tink. "For the time being, it will be your job to look after the girls."

Chapter 4

Oh, the unfairness! As soon as she was alone, Tink stomped her tiny foot in the air. Somehow she'd gotten stuck with the Clumsies. Tink would rather have had her wings dipped in mud!

"Why me?" she grumbled to herself. "Any other fairy would do just fine." But what could she do? It was the queen's command. So when Prilla decided to give the girls a tour, Tink had no choice but to follow along.

Prilla started her tour with the Home Tree, as any fairy would. The Home Tree was the heart of the fairies' world.

Earlier, the girls had been too excited to examine the tree properly. But now they saw all the details they'd missed. They marveled at the great knothole door, the sea-glass windows, and the tiny steps that wound around the trunk.

"Where do those go?" Gabby pointed to the different colored doors lining the tree's great branches. Some had crystal doorknobs or dandelion doormats. Others had silver wind chimes or sea-fan awnings hung above them.

"To the fairies' rooms. Each room is decorated according to its fairy's talent," Prilla explained.

"What kind of talent?" asked Lainey.

"Every kind!" said Prilla. "Every fairy in Pixie Hollow has a talent. It's the thing she does best and loves to do more than anything else. Look, there in the courtyard, that's a sweeping-talent fairy. And the one over there, carrying that plum—that's a harvest-talent fairy."

Kate giggled. *What funny talents!* she thought. "If I were a fairy, I'd have an exciting talent," she whispered to Mia.

Mia nodded. She was busy peering into the windows of the tearoom. Kate peeked over her shoulder. She saw a table made from the polished cross section of a tree trunk. It was set with plates and cups made from seashells. The napkins were folded flower petals.

"Everything is so pretty! I wish I could shrink myself and go inside," Mia said.

"Over here is Tink's workshop," Prilla said, leading the girls around the side of the tree.

Tink, who'd been sulking behind a tree root, looked up with a start. Her workshop was her pride and joy. She didn't want Clumsies poking around in there! She hurried over to keep an eye on them.

When Gabby saw Tink's workshop, she squealed with delight. "It's a teakettle!" she exclaimed. Sure enough, a real, human-sized teakettle had been squeezed between the Home Tree's roots. Its spout made a little awning over the tiny door.

"Tink's a tinker-talent fairy," Prilla explained. "The best in Pixie Hollow."

Normally, Tink would have been pleased by the compliment. But she was too busy watching Mia. The girl was down on her hands and knees, peeking in the window.

"Oh, look!" Mia cried. "There's a teeny-tiny workbench. And a bucket made from a thimble. Oh! And look at that chair made from an old bent spoon!"

"Let me see! Let me see!" cried Gabby, tugging at Mia's sleeve.

The other girls took turns peeping inside. They were so enthusiastic that finally even Tink had to smile.

"Isn't it just the cutest thing you've ever seen?" Mia exclaimed.

Tink's smile faded. Prilla looked embarrassed.

"What's wrong?" asked Mia.

"Fairies don't like to be called cute," Prilla said. "It's insulting."

"Oh, I didn't know. I'm sorry, Miss Tink," Mia said. Tink just rolled her eyes.

"Fairies don't say 'sorry,'" Prilla told Mia. "They say, 'I'd fly backward if I could.'"

Mia glanced at Tink and nodded, clearly afraid to say anything else at all.

"It's okay," Prilla said kindly. "When I

first got here, I didn't understand all the rules, either."

"What other rules are there?" Lainey asked.

"Well, for starters, fairies don't say Mister or Miss," Prilla explained. "And be careful who you tell secrets to. Fairies love to gossip! And another thing." Prilla lowered her voice. "Watch out for Vidia, the fast-flying-talent fairy. . . ."

Prilla kept talking, but Kate wasn't listening anymore. Rules had always bored her.

Kate looked around for something interesting. She spied a little building made of twigs. It had a straw roof and a wide door.

"What's this?" Kate asked, striding

over to it. She bent down to open the door.

"Don't!" cried Tink. "That's the—"

Frightened squeaks drowned out the rest of her words. A dozen mice burst through the door. They ran off in every direction.

"Oopsie," said Kate.

"That's the dairy mouse barn," Tink finished with a sigh.

"I'll help!" cried Lainey. She started

to chase after the mice. But she only frightened them more.

A fairy flew out of the barn. "You clumsy Clumsies!" she yelled.

"Maybe we'd better move on," Prilla said quickly, and hurried the girls away. When Kate glanced back over her shoulder, she saw the fairy herding the mice back into the barn.

Prilla led the girls through Pixie Hollow. They saw garden fairies watering flowers and caterpillar-shearing-talent fairies herding woolly caterpillars. Two fairies riding on the backs of squirrels chased each other through the trees.

"What are they doing?" asked Lainey.

"Playing tag," Prilla replied. "Those are animal-talent fairies."

Tink and Prilla took the girls to the

orchard, where the
harvest-talent fairies
gave them just-picked
peaches still warm
from the sun. Next, they
visited Havendish Stream. The
girls watched the water-talent fairies
sailing their leaf-boats.

Nearby, Kate saw a funny round
building. It was built from odd little
rocks. Going closer, she saw that they
weren't rocks, but peach pits.

"What's this place?" she asked.

"The mill," Prilla said, flying over. "It's
where we keep the fairy dust."

"What's fairy dust?" asked Lainey.

"It's what makes us sparkle," said a
voice nearby.

A sparrow man flew around the side

of the mill. He had floppy blond hair and a friendly smile. "The dust also helps us fly," he told the girls. "Without it, we can't fly more than a foot at a time."

"This is Terence," Prilla told the girls. "He's a dust talent."

"Would you like to see inside?" Terence asked them.

The girls crowded around the double doors. In the dim light, they could see a dozen pumpkin-canisters.

Terence lifted the lid off one of the pumpkins. The fairy dust was finer than flour. It shimmered with the colors of the rainbow.

"That's a lot of dust," Mia said.

"It's just enough," Terence replied. "In Pixie Hollow there's just enough of everything. No more, no less."

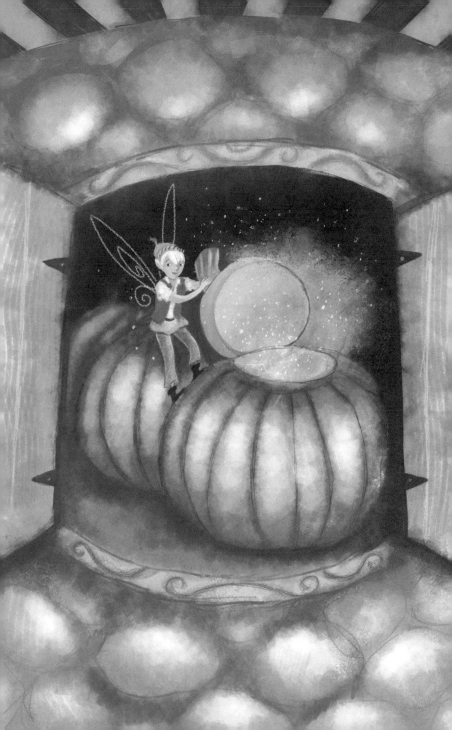

Kate was thinking about something Terence had said. "Fairy dust helps you fly. Could it help *us* fly, too?" she asked.

"Of course," Terence said. "Anyone can fly with fairy dust. In fact, that's how children usually get to Never Land. You're the first ones I've met to come on a blink."

Kate was startled by this news. "You mean, other kids have been here, too?"

"Oh, sure," said Terence. "Not very often, mind you. And usually they end up in other parts of Never Land. We don't see too many Clumsies in Pixie Hollow."

"So where are the kids now?" Mia wondered.

"Home," Tink said. The girls turned to her in surprise. It was the first time she'd spoken since the trouble at the mouse barn.

"Clumsies go home," Tink said again, matter-of-factly. "Unless they have no homes to go back to. Then they stay lost in Never Land forever."

The way she said "forever" sent a shiver down Kate's spine. "But," she said, "the ones who *do* go home, they come back to visit sometimes, don't they?"

"No, they don't," Tink said with a shrug. "They go home and grow up. And when they grow up, they forget. Never Land seems like something they once dreamed."

The girls were quiet, thinking about this. It was hard for them to imagine ever forgetting such a wonderful place.

"It's getting late," Prilla said, glancing at the sun. "We can see more of Pixie Hollow tomorrow."

"Come visit anytime," Terence told the girls as he shut the doors of the mill.

The setting sun turned the meadow gold as they made their way back to the Home Tree. It looked even more beautiful than when they'd first arrived in Pixie Hollow. But Kate barely saw it. Tink's words still troubled her.

Was it true that they would go home and forget about Never Land . . . or else stay here forever? To Kate, the choice—if it was a choice at all—seemed deeply unfair.

Well, I won't think about it, Kate told herself. After all, they were here now. There was still so much to do and see and discover.

Pushing the thought from her mind, Kate skipped ahead to join her friends.

chapter 5

"I can show you your room now," Prilla told the girls when they returned from the dust mill.

"We have a room?" Kate asked, surprised.

"Of course!" Prilla laughed. "Where did you think you'd sleep? On the ground?"

Kate wouldn't have minded. Sleeping outside, with nothing but the stars overhead, was something she'd always wanted to try.

"Come on," said Prilla, "the decorating-talent fairies are almost finished."

The last bit of light was draining from the sky. Kate, Mia, Lainey, and Gabby followed the fairies to a large weeping willow. Light shone beneath the willow's leaves, as if the tree glowed from within.

Tinker Bell parted the branches, and the girls stepped inside.

Kate gasped. It was the perfect room. Four girl-sized hammocks hung from the tree's branches. The willow's leaves spilled down around them like curtains. The velvety grass had been raked into pretty spiral patterns. Soft light came from lanterns set into notches in the tree's trunk.

Gabby looked closer at one of the lanterns. Half a dozen fireflies circled inside. "Lightning-bug lights!" she cried.

Mia sank down into one of the hammocks. It had been filled with moss and covered with silk sheets to make a sort of swinging bed. She lifted a pillow to her face and sniffed. "It smells like roses."

"It's stuffed with rose petals," Prilla said. "Do you like it?"

"It's the most beautiful room I've ever seen," Mia replied.

The girls noticed two tiny hammocks hanging next to theirs. "Do you live here, too?" Gabby asked the fairies hopefully.

"Tink and I have our own rooms in the Home Tree," Prilla explained. "But we thought we should stay with you, for now, anyway."

On another branch, Lainey discovered

a basin made from tightly woven banana leaves. It was filled with cool springwater. The girls washed their faces, and cleaned their teeth with licorice twigs. The sewing-talent fairies had made nightgowns for them by stitching together flannel sheets. The girls slipped these over their heads, shivering at the softness.

As they climbed into their beds, Tink went around tapping the lanterns to put the fireflies out.

"Leave one on," Mia said. "At home, Mami always leaves a light on for Gabby."

"Oh!" Lainey gasped and sat up. "Home!"

Until that moment, the girls had not

thought once of their parents. But now, as if waking from a dream, they realized how long they'd been gone.

"Our moms and dads are going to be so worried!" said Mia.

"They're going to be so *angry*," Kate added grimly.

"If only there were a way we could send a message. Just to let them know we're all right," said Lainey.

Tink, who was examining Gabby's wings, looked up. "Prilla could take a note," she said.

"That's right—I could blink there! Oh, Tink, you're so clever," said Prilla.

Tink shrugged and turned back to the wings. She had been alarmed when Gabby took them off and hung them on a twig. But now she saw that they were made of cloth and wire. Not real fairy wings at all.

The girls got busy preparing their message. Kate declared that Mia should write it, since she had the best handwriting. The fairies had no pens or paper. Mia wrote on a strip of birch bark using a twig dipped in berry ink.

Dear Mami and Papi,
How are you? We are fine. We are
visiting in Never Land. It's nice here.
Please tell the other moms don't worry.
Love, Mia   Gabby   Lainey   Kate

Mia fanned the wet ink. When it was dry, she gave the note to Prilla. Prilla held the rolled-up bark in her arms. She pictured a tunnel with Mia and Gabby's house at the end of it.

She blinked.

Prilla was in a dark room. She could hear soft snores. Looking down, she saw a sleeping boy holding a stuffed dinosaur.

Wrong house! Prilla blinked again.

She was sitting on the pages of an open book. A boy and a girl stared down at her. "Look, Mom! A fairy!" cried the girl.

"No, it's a picture of a bird. See?" Their mother's finger landed on the page next to Prilla. She blinked away.

On her third blink, Prilla found herself on the doorstep of a narrow brick house. It looked like Mia and Gabby's house, as far as Prilla could remember. Prilla placed the note on the doorstep. Then she blinked away—too soon to see the wind pick up the note and carry it off.

"I did it!" she exclaimed as she arrived back in the willow room.

"Did what?" asked Kate.

"I delivered the note," Prilla said. "I didn't mean to be gone so long. It took a while to find the right house."

"But you've been right here the whole time," said Kate. To the girls, no more than an instant had passed. Prilla hadn't even left the room.

Prilla was surprised to hear this. She had never thought about what a blink looked like from the other side.

"Do you think it might be like that for us?" Lainey asked after a moment. "Do you think back at home no time has passed since we left?"

Prilla considered Lainey's question. "Maybe so," she said. "A blink is a blink, whichever way you go."

A sigh of relief went around the room. As soon as they were sure their parents wouldn't be worried, the girls' mood lifted.

"This is like a sleepover!" said Lainey, snuggling under the covers.

"It's better," Mia said. "We can stay up all night if we want!"

But it had been a long day, full of

surprises. Soon enough, their giggles gave way to yawns. One by one, Gabby, Lainey, and Mia dropped off to sleep.

*

Kate lay awake for a long time. She was too excited to sleep. All her life she had secretly believed that something extraordinary would happen to her. Now it finally had, and she didn't want to miss a single moment.

When she was sure everyone else was asleep, Kate threw back the covers and crept out of bed. Standing on tiptoe, she peeped into Prilla's and Tink's hammocks. They were asleep, too.

Quietly, Kate parted the willow branches and stepped outside.

If Pixie Hollow was enchanting by day,

it was even more so at night. Lanterns glowed softly in the trees. A warm breeze stirred up the scent of jasmine.

Kate made her way toward the meadow, the grass deliciously cool under her bare feet. She threw her arms wide and spun with joy. Today had been marvelous. And who knew what tomorrow would bring? There were no parents or teachers here, no rules or restrictions. Nothing but days and days of adventure ahead . . .

A laugh rang out from the darkness. Kate looked around. "Who's there?" she whispered.

A cricket's chirp was the only reply.

A cloud crossed the moon. Kate shivered and wrapped her arms around herself. *I'm imagining things,* she thought.

But the night seemed darker now. Turning, Kate started quickly back to the willow, brushing past a primrose bush. In her hurry, she didn't notice the pair of eyes gleaming at her from within its branches.

Chapter 6

When the girls awoke the next morning, they found a basket of freshly baked muffins waiting for them outside the willow tree. Tucked inside the basket was a note from Queen Clarion.

The note was written in Leaf Lettering, the secret fairy alphabet. Tink read it for the girls. "'You're to come to the fairy circle this morning,'" Tink said. "The queen has news."

"The fairy circle!" Prilla exclaimed. "It must be something important."

After breakfast, Prilla and Tink led the way across the meadow. It was another sparkling day. The sky was robin's-egg blue, and the grass smelled fresh with dew. The girls laughed and chatted as they walked.

But when they reached a little clearing in the woods, they got quiet. Around a hawthorn tree, a ring of toadstools sprouted from the mossy ground. A hushed feeling hung in the air. The girls could tell it was a magical place.

Queen Clarion was seated on a snow-white toadstool. On either side of her sat a fairy.

"This is Rain, a weather-talent fairy," said Queen Clarion, introducing the fairy

on her left. "Rain knows all there is to know about the weather of Never Land. And this is Skye, a seeing talent." Queen Clarion nodded to the other fairy. "Skye can see things the rest of us can't. She and Rain have news about how you came to Never Land."

Rain stepped forward. "A southern puff was bellowing," she said. "Cold highwilds drove the isle mainlandish—"

"What she means," Skye broke in, "is that we think Never Land rode the waves all the way to your home."

"Waves? You mean like the ocean?" asked Kate. Skye nodded.

"But that's impossible," said Mia. "We don't live near an ocean."

"Nothing's impossible," Skye said. "The island does what it wants. We think it came so close to your world that it only took the tiniest tug to bring you here."

"My blink!" Prilla realized.

"Exactly," said Skye. "I want to show you something."

From behind a toadstool, she dragged out an old pair of spectacles. The lenses were foggy. The wire rims were bent. The glasses clearly had seen much better days.

"Glasses?" asked Kate. She had been expecting something more exciting.

"I found these washed up on the beach one day," Skye explained. "I fixed them with a little fairy magic. Step inside the fairy circle and try them on."

As usual, Kate stepped forward first.

She stood in the middle of the ring of toadstools. She put on the glasses. Instead of seeing the forest in front of her, she saw a familiar front door. "I can see my house!" she cried.

The other girls tried the glasses, too. They all saw their own homes. "But why does it look so misty?" Lainey asked.

"The glasses tell you how close to the mainland you are. The farther away you are, the harder it is to see," Skye said.

"When will we be close again?" Mia asked.

Rain held up something that looked like a pinwheel. It spun in the breeze. "Elephoons running north," she said, watching the wheel spin. "Could be as soon as sun-twixt."

"What she *means*," Skye said, "is that it might be very soon. Between the next sunrise and sunset, in fact." When the girls looked puzzled, she added, "Prilla can blink you home tomorrow."

"Tomorrow?" Tink said, perking up. That meant her days of Clumsy-sitting were almost over. She could go back to her workshop! Tink couldn't help herself—she clicked her heels with joy.

Kate looked around at her friends. Their unhappy faces mirrored what she was feeling. "But we just *got* here," she said. "Do we have to leave already?"

"It might be your only chance," said Skye. "We don't know when Never Land will drift that way again."

"Skye and Rain, you've been very helpful," Queen Clarion told them. The two fairies nodded to the queen. Then they flew away.

As the girls left the fairy circle, Kate felt as if she might cry. *It's not fair,* she thought. *We haven't even had an adventure yet.*

"Well, what would you like to do on your last day in Pixie Hollow?" Prilla asked. She tried to make her voice light, although she felt as sad as the girls did. She was sorry to see them go so soon.

"We could go blueberry picking? Or leaf-boat racing? Or maybe wild mushroom hunting?"

"Flying," Kate said. She hadn't even known she was going to say it. The word popped out of her mouth. But once it had, she knew it with all her heart. "I want to fly."

"Yes!" Mia agreed, her face brightening.

"I want to fly, too!" said Lainey.

"Me three!" said Gabby.

"Gabby, you're too little—" Mia began. But Gabby gave her such a glare that Mia shut her mouth.

"We want to learn to fly," Kate repeated. "All of us."

Prilla looked at Tink, who shrugged. "I don't see why not," Tink said. "I'll ask if Terence can spare some fairy dust."

All the girls cheered.

Kate cheered loudest of all, because a plan was starting to form in her mind. It was a crazy, brilliant plan—a plan for returning to Never Land.

Chapter 7

For their flying lesson, Tink led the girls to a bend in the stream. The ground here was carpeted with soft moss. Tree branches formed a canopy overhead.

"It's a good place to learn," Tink said. "Plenty of branches to catch yourself on, and a nice soft landing."

Terence had come along with them and had brought a small sack of fairy dust. "Who's first?" he asked the girls.

"Me!" said Kate. She watched as Terence

measured out a tiny fairy cupful of dust. "That's all we get?" It didn't look like enough dust to make her fly. It hardly looked like enough to make her sneeze.

"Fairy dust is precious," Tink said. "Everyone gets a cupful a day. No more, no less. Hold your breath now. You don't want any blowing away."

Kate held her breath as Terence poured the dust over her. At once, she felt a tingle from the tips of her ears to her toes. It felt like warming up next to a fire after a day of playing in the snow. She flapped her arms, but nothing happened.

"Now what?" she asked.

"Patience," said Tink. Terence was pouring dust over the other girls.

"Ooh!" Prilla fluttered up and down. "This is so exciting!"

"Think of something light," Tink said. "Wriggle your shoulders. Bounce on your toes."

The girls concentrated. They wriggled. They bounced. And then . . .

"Oh my gosh!" Mia squealed. Her feet were leaving the ground. "Gabby, hold on!" Mia clutched her little sister's hand and together they rose into the air.

"Look at me! I'm flying!" Lainey cried, floating up next to them.

Kate still wasn't moving. She pushed off the ground—hard—and shot high into the air. "Hey! Look at meeee— Ow!" Kate bonked her head on a tree branch. Clutching her head, she sank back down to the ground.

"Meow?" Lainey giggled as she floated by. "You sound like a cat, Kate."

Kate scowled and rubbed her head. Gabby bobbed past, her wings fluttering in the breeze. "Come on, Kate. It's fun," she said. She turned a shaky somersault in the air. "Wheeeee!"

Kate pushed off again. But instead of going up, she went sideways. "Ooof!" she grunted as she hit a tree trunk. She landed on the ground again.

Above her, Mia was swimming gracefully through the air. Kate watched her jealously. Mia looked like a mermaid, with her long hair streaming out behind her.

Kate scowled. *Why can't I fly like that?* At home, she was usually the one who was good at things.

Maybe I'm not trying hard enough. Kate closed her eyes. She thought of light

things—feathers, clouds, dandelion fluff. She thought so hard she gave herself a headache.

"I can see the whole world!" Mia cried from somewhere above her.

Kate gritted her teeth. "Concentrate!" she told herself. She pushed off again. This time she rose higher . . . and higher. . . .

"I did it!" cried Kate. "I'm flying!"

She was headed right toward Mia. *Why is Mia holding on to that tree branch?* Kate wondered.

At the last second, Kate noticed Mia's pale face. She saw how tightly Mia was gripping the branch. She realized that Mia was terrified.

But it was too late. Kate couldn't stop. She crashed into Mia, who let go of the branch. They both screamed as they started to fall.

"Think of flying!" Tink shouted at them. *"Believe* you can fly!" But the girls couldn't think of anything but the ground speeding toward them.

Kate smacked into Lainey on the way down. Now all three were falling.

Splash!

Splash!

Splash!

One after another, the girls landed in Havendish Stream.

Gabby was still doing air-somersaults. But seeing the older girls fall, she fell, too. Gabby always wanted to do what the big kids did. She landed in the stream right next to Kate. *Splash!*

The girls were soaked. They were shivering. "Thanks a lot, Kate," Mia said through chattering teeth.

Just then, they heard a high, silvery sound, like little bells ringing. It was Tink laughing. The girls stared, astonished. They'd never heard Tink laugh before.

"I think," Tink said, wiping her eyes, "that's enough flying for one day."

*

Kate was quiet on the way back to Pixie Hollow. She walked slowly behind the other girls, thinking.

Terence had said that other kids had once flown to Never Land with Peter Pan. If that was true, Kate and her friends could fly there, too. That was Kate's plan— to come back to Never Land whenever she wished. Just because other kids hadn't come back didn't mean it wasn't possible.

For Kate's plan to work, though, she had to learn to fly. But she hadn't flown—not for more than a moment, anyway. Certainly not well enough to fly across an ocean.

And now it was too late. Tomorrow they had to go home and leave Pixie Hollow behind—maybe forever.

The more Kate thought, the more slowly she walked. The more slowly she walked, the more she fell behind. At some point, Kate realized she could no longer hear her friends' voices.

She stopped and looked around. She wasn't sure which way to go.

"Hello?" she called uncertainly. "Hey, guys?"

The leaves of a bush nearby rustled. Kate spun around. She remembered she was in a strange forest. Who knew what kind of creatures lived there?

Kate picked up a big stick. Holding it like a sword, she faced the bush.

Out flew a fairy.

Kate sighed, relieved. "Just a fairy!"

"Yes, clever one, I'm a fairy." The fairy had long black hair and a pale, pinched face. Her wings were narrow and pointed like knives. "Are you planning to bash me with that stick?" she asked Kate.

Kate lowered the stick. "What are you doing here?" she asked.

"I go where I please, darling," the fairy said with a sniff. "What are *you* doing here? And why are you all wet?"

Kate looked down at her damp clothes. "We had a flying lesson," she said. "It didn't go very well."

The fairy smirked. "Clumsies can't fly. They don't have wings!"

"My friends don't have wings and *they* flew," Kate pointed out.

"Is that so? Then I guess you simply have no talent," the fairy said.

"I guess not," Kate agreed sadly.

"Although, if you *really* want to fly, I might be able to help you," the fairy said.

"How?" asked Kate.

"Well, sweet, I *am* the best fast flier in Pixie Hollow." As if to prove it, the fairy buzzed a circle around Kate's head.

A flying-talent fairy! Kate's heartbeat quickened. She noticed how this fairy's wings sliced the air as she flew. Other fairies fluttered. "You'd really help me?" Kate asked.

"I could. Though I'd need your help in return," the fairy said slyly.

"Of course," Kate agreed.

"Then meet me at moonrise in the orchard. By the sour-plum tree." The fairy turned to leave.

"Wait!" Kate called. "What's your name?"

The fairy glanced back. "Vidia."

Somewhere in the back of Kate's mind, the name rang a bell. But she hadn't been listening when Prilla warned them about Vidia. "My name's Kate," she said.

Vidia shrugged as if Kate's name was not important. She started away.

"Oh! Wait!" Kate called. "How do I get back to . . ." She trailed off. Vidia was already gone.

Just then, Tink flew up. "There you are!" she cried when she saw Kate. "We've been looking for you." She looked around. "Who were you talking to?"

"It was—nothing. Nobody," said Kate. For some reason she didn't want to tell

Tink about her flying lesson with Vidia.

Tink's brow furrowed. But to Kate's relief, she didn't ask any more questions. "Well, come on, then," Tink said. "The other girls are waiting."

Even Tink's scowl didn't dampen Kate's spirits. She was going to learn to fly— from the fastest flier in Pixie Hollow!

Chapter 8

That night, after her friends fell asleep, Kate sneaked out of the willow room. At the edge of the orchard, she spotted a bent tree with twisted branches. Right away she knew it was the sour-plum tree.

"Vidia?" Kate whispered. A moment later, she felt a tiny breeze as Vidia flew up beside her.

"I'm ready for my flying lesson," Kate told her.

"First things first, dearest. We need fairy dust." Vidia held out something that resembled a man's sock.

Kate looked closer. It *was* a man's sock. It was long and red with a stitched-up hole in the toe. "I took it from a pirate," Vidia told her. "Don't worry, I washed it."

"What's it for?" asked Kate.

"To carry the dust, clever one! Now go ahead. Fill it up."

"The whole thing?" Kate was shocked. The sock was as long as her forearm. "Tink says everyone only gets a cupful."

Vidia smirked. "Tink doesn't care about flying. Not like *we* do."

"But—"

"Use your head, sweetness. If a tiny cup of dust helps you fly, think how much faster you'd go with more."

Kate took the sock. "Why can't you get the dust yourself?" she asked.

"Dearest, if we stand around talking all night long, there will be no time for flying," Vidia said. "Now off you go."

As Kate started away, Vidia added, "Don't worry, fairy dust belongs to us all."

Kate walked along the stream toward the mill. She felt funny. It didn't seem right to take fairy dust in the middle of the night. It seemed like stealing.

But Vidia said fairy dust belongs to everyone, Kate reminded herself. Besides, she would need extra fairy dust for all her friends to fly back to Never Land, too.

Ahead, in the moonlight, she could see

the mill. Kate tiptoed closer. She hoped Terence was there. Then she could just ask for the fairy dust.

"Hello?" Kate whispered. "Anyone here?"

The only sound was the *splish-splash* of the waterwheel turning in the stream.

Kate tried the big double doors. They opened easily. Through them, she could just make out the shapes of the pumpkin-canisters.

Kate was too big to crawl inside. But she could easily fit her arm through the door. She reached in and pulled a pumpkin toward her. Taking off its lid, she saw that it was three-quarters full. The dust glittered faintly in the moonlight.

Kate dipped her hand in and pulled

out a fistful . . . and another and another.
In the end, it took most of the dust in the
pumpkin to fill the sock.

Fairy dust belongs to everyone, Kate told
herself again. She put the canister back
and closed the doors.

As she stood, she noticed that her
hands were sparkly with dust. She could

feel its magic already starting. She half ran, half flew all the way to the sour-plum tree.

Vidia grinned when she saw the filled sock. She scooped out a big portion for herself, then one for Kate. When she was done, Kate tied the sock through a belt loop in her jeans.

"All right. Follow me," Vidia said, and dove into the air.

Kate sprang after her. The extra fairy dust made her feel powerful. In a flash, she was high above the sour-plum tree.

But a second later, she started to sink. She tried to think of light things, as Tink had told her to do. But the ground was coming fast. . . .

"You're trying too hard," Vidia whispered into her ear. She was hovering next to Kate. "Think, but don't think. Hold the idea lightly in your mind. Feel the air lift you."

Kate tried to think and *not* think about flying. She felt the night air on her bare arms. She pushed against it and rose up . . . up. . . .

In an instant, Kate was higher than the Home Tree. She swooped through the air. Cool air rushed against her face. She was flying!

How could this have ever been hard? she wondered. It seemed so easy now.

Kate found that she could use her arms like rudders to turn. She dipped down and felt leaves brush against her toes. She shot up through the air again and made a loop.

"You've got it, child! Now try going

faster!" Vidia sped ahead. Kate chased after her.

"Faster!" Vidia shrieked. Kate sped up again. She was flying faster than she'd ever thought she could.

But Vidia flew faster still, so fast she looked like a shooting star in the night. Kate could hear her tiny voice crying, "Faster! Faster!"

Kate laughed with joy. Below her, Never Land lay spread out like a patchwork quilt. Light patches of sand and rock were mixed with darker patches of trees. Above, stars glittered coldly in the velvet black sky.

"Where should we go?" she shouted to Vidia.

"Anywhere!" came the faint reply.

In the distance, Kate saw a tall mountain. She aimed herself toward it.

Suddenly, a large shape burst out at her. Two yellow eyes flashed in the darkness. Kate screamed and threw her hands in front of her face. She dropped in the air, just missing the owl.

The bird screeched its annoyance at her, then flapped away.

Kate regained her balance. "That was a close one," she said in a shaky voice. She was trembling all over. "Can we stop for a minute? Vidia?"

There was no answer. She scanned the sky, but she didn't see Vidia's glow.

Kate looked down. Her belt loop was empty. Vidia was gone—and so was the rest of the fairy dust.

Chapter 9

Tink sat on the bench in her workshop. Sunlight gleamed off the saucepan as she studied the crack in its handle. "A tricky fix," she murmured. "Very tricky—"

"Tink!" a voice interrupted.

"Not now," Tink told it. "I'm busy."

"Tink!" the voice insisted. "Wake up!"

Tink opened her eyes. She wasn't in her workshop. She was in a hammock in the willow room. Mia and Gabby were staring down at her.

Tink frowned at them. "I was having the nicest dream," she said.

"Prilla told us to wake you," Mia said. "Kate's gone."

Tink sat up and yawned. "Maybe she went for a walk."

Mia shook her head. "We asked around. Nobody in Pixie Hollow has seen her."

Never a moment's peace with these Clumsies, Tink thought with a sigh. *But at least it will be over soon.* Today the girls would return to their own homes, and Tink could go back to her workshop. Just the thought of it filled her with energy. She hopped out of bed. "All right. Let's find her," she said.

Outside, they met up with Prilla and Lainey. "We just came from the beach," said Prilla. "We didn't see Kate there, either."

"Well, it's still early," Tink said. "She can't have gone very far."

Just then, they saw Terence coming toward them. Right away, Tink knew something was wrong. Terence's wings sagged, and his glow was dim.

"What's the matter?" Tink asked, concerned.

"Someone stole some fairy dust from the mill," Terence said.

"Vidia!" Prilla said with a gasp. "But how did she get it?" Vidia had stolen dust before, more than once. Because of this, she could no longer go near the mill. The queen had used fairy magic to make sure of it.

But Terence shook his head. "It wasn't

Vidia. Not this time. You'd better come see this." He glanced at Mia, Lainey, and Gabby, adding, "You come, too."

They followed Terence downstream to the mill. A pumpkin-canister was sitting outside its doors. Terence lifted the lid. "This was full yesterday."

Tink and Prilla looked inside. Only a thin dusting—not even a cupful—remained in the bottom.

"A Clumsy stole the rest," Terence said, looking hard at the girls.

"You think *we* stole it?" Lainey squeaked, stunned.

"We didn't steal anything!" Mia said. Her dark eyes flashed. She put her arm around Gabby protectively.

"Then explain this," said Terence. He pointed to the mill door. There, outlined

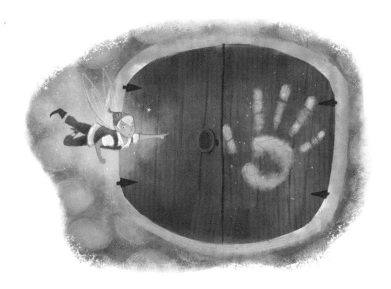

in fairy dust, was a girl-sized handprint.

The girls looked at each other with round eyes. "You don't suppose . . . ?" Lainey began.

"Kate wouldn't steal," Mia said. But she didn't sound certain.

"Kate's missing," Tink explained to Terence. "Since last night."

"If she took the fairy dust, she could be on the other side of Never Land by now," he said. "It could take days to find her."

"Today's the day the girls are supposed to go home!" Prilla said. She turned to Tink. "What should we do?"

Tink tugged on her bangs. She thought of the saucepan waiting in her workshop. Then she looked around at the girls' worried faces. She imagined Kate, lost in Never Land. Suddenly, the saucepan didn't seem so important.

"Gather up all the fairies you can find," Tink told Prilla. "Kate's somewhere out there." She swept an arm toward the forest. "It may take all of Pixie Hollow to find her."

*

Prilla hurried to tell the messenger-talent fairies about Kate. The messengers alerted the scouts. Within minutes, the scouts had fanned out across the forest, searching for a sign of the lost girl.

The water-talent fairies joined the search, too. They paddled their leaf-boats along Havendish Stream, calling Kate's name up and down the banks.

Meanwhile, animal-talent fairies took to the skies. They rode on the backs of blue jays and starlings. They circled high in the air, hoping to catch a glimpse of Kate.

Prilla waited at the Home Tree with Mia, Lainey, and Gabby. Tink hadn't wanted them to join the search. "You can't get far walking," she'd said. "And it's too easy to get lost in the forest if you don't know the way."

"I want to fly and look for Kate, too," Gabby said as they watched the fairies fly high above them.

"We can't," Mia told her. "There isn't any extra fairy dust for us to fly with. Kate took it."

Gabby stuck out her lower lip. "That's not fair."

"No, it isn't," Mia agreed with a frown.

"Anyway," Gabby said, "I don't need fairy dust to fly. I can use my wings."

"Mia, you don't think Kate left us on purpose, do you?" Lainey asked.

"I don't know," Mia said, her frown deepening. It was clear she'd been thinking the same thing.

Lainey squinted up at the sun. It was high in the sky now. The day was passing quickly. "What will we do if we can't find

Kate before we have to leave?" she asked.

Nobody answered. No one knew. "We'll find her," Prilla said at last, trying to sound confident. "All of Pixie Hollow is out looking for her now."

"Where's Gabby?" Lainey said suddenly.

"What do you mean?" asked Mia. "She was right here a second ago."

The girls and Prilla looked all around the Home Tree. Then they looked around the trees nearby. Lainey even ran back to the willow room to check. There was no sign of Gabby.

"I should have been watching her," Mia said. "Where could she be?"

"She said she wanted to fly," Lainey remembered. "You don't think she went looking for Kate, do you?"

"She can't fly," Prilla said. "She doesn't have any fairy dust."

"But she *believes* she can fly," Mia said.

They all turned toward the forest. "Oh, no," Prilla said. "Now we have *two* lost girls."

*

Tink and her friend Beck, an animal-talent fairy, were sweeping over the forest on the back of a starling. It was their third pass that morning. But they still hadn't spotted Kate.

"Do you think she could have gotten as far as Torth Mountain?" Beck shouted over the rushing wind.

Tink stared at the tall mountain in the distance. It was hard to say how far away it was, or whether Kate might have reached

it. Never Land was always changing in size. That was part of the island's magic. Sometimes it might take days to cross it. Other times it might take only hours.

"I guess we could have a look," Tink said with a last glance at the forest.

Just then, something shiny on the ground caught Tink's eye. She looked closer. At first she thought it was a giant dragonfly. Then she realized it was Gabby's shiny wings.

How in the name of Never Land did she get all the way out here? Tink wondered.

Tink didn't know it, but Never Land was exactly how Gabby had gotten there. The island had felt Gabby's belief. It had shrunk itself to help the little girl.

Gabby looked up and spotted the

fairies. She waved her hands and shouted something.

Tink and Beck swooped closer on their bird. Finally, they heard what Gabby was shouting.

"I found Kate! I did! I found her!" Gabby pointed to a nearby tree.

And there, Tink saw, was Kate, tangled high up among its branches.

chapter 10

Once Kate had been found, Tink and Beck sent a call out to the rest of the fairies. Everyone, including Mia and Lainey, hurried to the big oak tree. They could all see Kate high in the branches. She looked tired and scared.

Of course, the next problem was how to get her down. Luckily, this was just the sort of problem Tink enjoyed solving. After much tinkering, she rigged up a pulley system. She made the pulley herself, using old mouse-cart wheels. The harvest fairies attached it to the highest branches. Then everyone helped to hoist Kate down.

On the ground, Kate hugged her friends. When she heard that Gabby was the one who'd found her, she gave the little girl an extra hug. Kate told them about her flying lesson with Vidia and how she'd ended up in the tree.

"When I couldn't find Vidia, I got scared. I tried to land, but it was dark. I couldn't see where I was going, and I crashed into the oak tree," she explained. "I couldn't fly anymore, either. I guess I'd used up my fairy dust."

"Why didn't you use the dust you took from the mill?" Terence asked.

"It's gone," Kate said. "I had it tied to my belt loop, but now it's missing."

"Vidia took it, I bet," Tink said.

"So that's what Vidia was up to," Prilla said with a frown. "She got Kate to steal dust from the mill so she could have it all for herself."

Kate was shocked. "I didn't steal! Vidia said . . ."

Kate trailed off. From the looks on her friends' faces, she knew that Vidia hadn't told her the truth. "I wouldn't have taken it if I had known it was stealing," she said. "I just wanted to learn how to fly. I thought if we all knew how to fly, we could find our way back to Pixie Hollow."

"You wanted to come back?" Prilla asked.

"More than anything," Kate said. The other girls nodded. "But now I've gone and messed it all up, haven't I?"

To her surprise, Tink flew over and landed on her shoulder. To Kate, it felt as if a butterfly were resting there. "You haven't messed anything up," Tink said. "And you might find your way back here still. I would be glad to see you."

"Oh!" Prilla said then. "Look how late it's getting! If we don't go now, we may miss our chance to get you to the mainland!"

The sun was low in the sky. It was time for the girls to go to the fairy circle—and then home.

✳

Before they could leave, though, they had to say good-bye to Queen Clarion. They found her waiting for them at the fairy circle. She was perched on the snow-white toadstool, looking as queenly as ever.

One by one, the girls said their good-byes. Kate stepped forward last.

"I'm sorry I lost all your fairy dust," she said to the queen.

"We'll get it back—most of it, anyway,"

Queen Clarion replied. "Vidia will return eventually. Pixie Hollow is her home. No Never fairy can stay away for long."

That made Kate feel a little better. There were many other things she wanted to say about how much she loved Pixie Hollow and Havendish Stream and the orchard and the willow room and all the fairies she'd met. Instead, she said, "Thanks for being so nice to us."

The queen smiled and said, "You are always welcome in Pixie Hollow." She held out her tiny hand. Ever so gently, Kate grasped it between her thumb and forefinger and shook it.

Kate stepped into the center of the fairy circle, where her friends and Prilla were waiting. Rain was there with her funny little pinwheel. "The tide is

forwarding. Mark is aflay," she said.

"She means," said Skye, "it's time to go."

The girls joined hands. Prilla landed on Gabby's upturned palm. They were all together, just as they had been when they arrived in Never Land.

"Bye-bye, fairies!" Gabby shouted.

The other girls joined her. "Good-bye! Good-bye!" they called.

"Fly safely!" The queen and Terence waved. Tink just reached for her bangs. Not because she was annoyed this time, but because she wanted to hide her misty eyes.

Then Prilla blinked, and the world blinked, too.

But when the girls opened their eyes, nothing had changed. They were still standing in the fairy circle.

"It didn't work," Kate murmured.

"What?" Rain frowned and shook her pinwheel. Then she said a lot of jingly things the girls couldn't understand.

"She means," said Skye, looking embarrassed, "that we may have made an error or two."

But the girls were all smiling. "It didn't work," Kate said again, more loudly. "We don't have to go home! Not just yet."

The girls stood hand in hand. Tink fluttered over and landed on Kate's shoulder. Together, they watched the sun sink below the horizon.

Not one of them doubted that they would make it home someday. But in the meantime, they had many adventures ahead of them in Never Land.

Read this Sneak peek of The Space Between, the next Never Girls adventure!

Lainey Winters was soaring.

For a brief moment, her heart seemed to stop. The ground fell away, and she rose up, up, up . . . and over the fallen log.

An instant later, she touched down again, bounding through the forest on the back of a doe. Trees flashed by in a blur of green. Lainey dug her hands deeper into the doe's fur. She held on tight as they darted around bushes and flew over stones.

Leaves crashed above. Lainey looked up and saw a squirrel racing through the trees. A tiny fairy sat on its back, her long brown braid swinging behind her. The squirrel leaped from branch to branch, keeping pace with the doe.

Lainey leaned forward, urging her doe on. The fairy did the same.

Ahead was a small clearing. In its center stood a tall maple tree, bigger than any other tree in the forest. From a distance, its branches seemed to sparkle and move. This was due to the many fairies who hummed around it like bees around a honeycomb. The maple was called the

Home Tree, and it was the heart of Pixie Hollow, the Never fairies' world.

Lainey steered the doe toward the Home Tree. Even without looking up, she could sense the fairy on the squirrel following above.

A few feet from the tree, the squirrel shot past Lainey. It landed on a branch and came to a stop just as Lainey and the doe pulled up at the Home Tree's roots.

Lainey laughed. "You beat me again, Fawn!" she called to the fairy on the squirrel.

"I wouldn't be much of an animal-talent fairy if I couldn't win a race against a Clumsy, would I?" Fawn replied, smiling.

Lainey slid off the doe's back, pushing the big glasses she wore up her nose. She didn't care about winning or losing. For her, the joy was in riding the deer, feeling it turn when she wanted to turn, knowing when it would leap. In her real life, the one where she went to school and lived with her parents, Lainey had never even had a pet, not so much as a goldfish. But here in Never Land, she'd played hide-and-seek with wild hares. She'd listened to the songs of loons. She'd cradled baby hedgehogs in her hand. Things she'd never dreamed possible seemed to happen every day.